Disney
DUMBO

This is the story of a little elephant with a big heart, and two very big ears, who learned to soar.

Printed in the U.S.A • ISBN: 1-61524-328-3
Disney Handle Box Set Book - Dumbo • 10 11 12 13 B&M 35652 10 9 8 7 6 5 4 3 2

It was morning at the circus. Hopeful mothers looked up as storks flew overhead. Each stork carried a tiny bundle that held a baby animal.

Mrs. Jumbo sighed as she watched the happy mothers cuddling their babies. "Oh, dear. I did so hope there would be a bundle for me," she thought.

A stork flew into Mrs. Jumbo's railway car and dropped a large bundle. Inside was a baby elephant. "Jumbo Junior" is what Mrs. Jumbo named him. "Look at him!" cried the other elephants excitedly. "Isn't he a *darling*?"

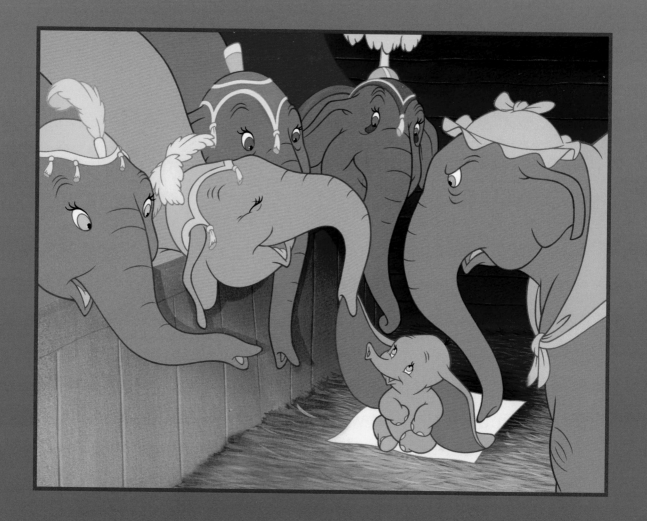

Just then, Mrs. Jumbo's baby sneezed.
Out flapped two *enormous* ears!
The other elephants gasped. Then they began to giggle.
"Aren't they funny!" said one elephant.
"Dumbo!" said another.

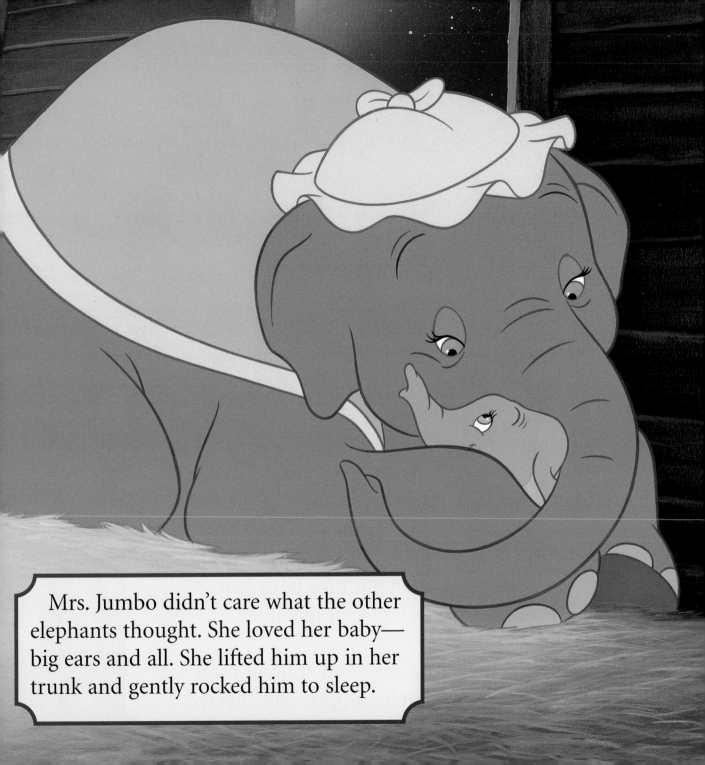

Mrs. Jumbo didn't care what the other elephants thought. She loved her baby—big ears and all. She lifted him up in her trunk and gently rocked him to sleep.

That night, the circus train stopped and all the animals climbed out. The circus men put up a huge tent.

The next morning, the circus parade made its way through the town.

The band played. The clowns and animals marched down the street as the people clapped and cheered.

Crowds hurried to the circus tent that night. They were eager to see all the animals.

"Look at his ears!" cried one noisy boy, pointing at Dumbo. They were the funniest things he'd ever seen.

The boys laughed and teased Dumbo. Then one of them pulled the little elephant's ears.

Mrs. Jumbo trumpeted with
anger. When she raised a hay bale to
throw at the naughty boys, they ran away in terror.
"Down! Down!" cried the Ringmaster,
cracking his whip.
Dumbo's mother was taken away and locked
in a small cage, far away from Dumbo.

Back in the tent, the other elephants gossiped about Dumbo's mother.

"I think she went a bit too far," one said.

"It's all the fault of—" They pointed to Dumbo—then turned their backs on him.

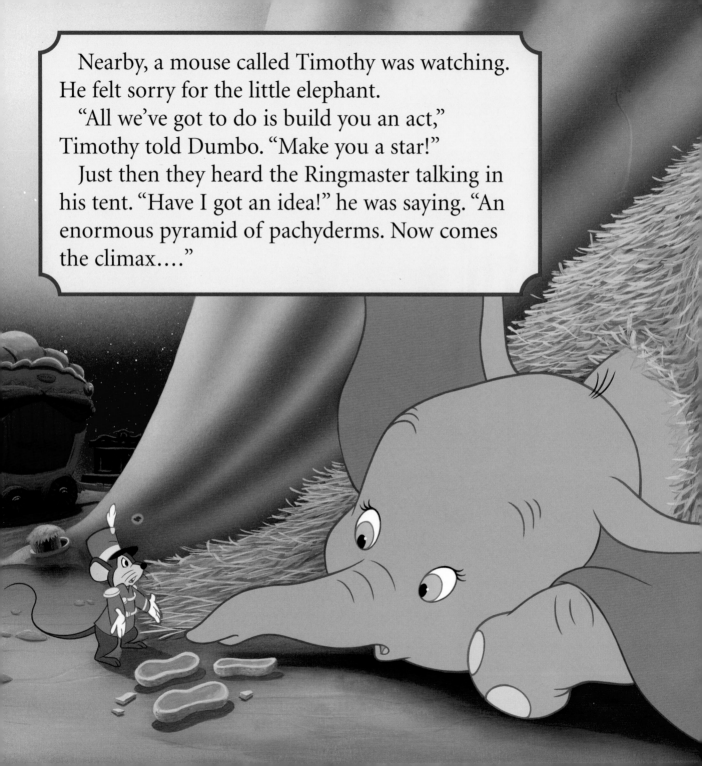

Nearby, a mouse called Timothy was watching. He felt sorry for the little elephant.

"All we've got to do is build you an act," Timothy told Dumbo. "Make you a star!"

Just then they heard the Ringmaster talking in his tent. "Have I got an idea!" he was saying. "An enormous pyramid of pachyderms. Now comes the climax...."

So, as soon as the Ringmaster was asleep, Timothy crept into his tent. He scampered up to the Ringmaster's ear and said, "Who is your climax? The little elephant with the big ears—Dumbo!"

"Dumbo…," mumbled the Ringmaster, "Dumbo…"

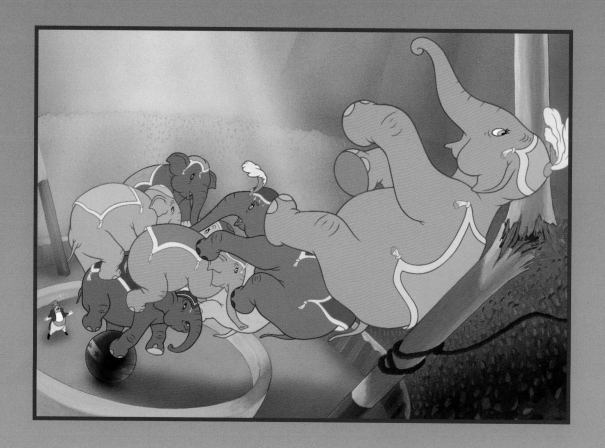

The next morning, the Ringmaster tried out his new idea. He had all the elephants balance carefully on top of one another. And Dumbo was to be the very top elephant—the star!

But when Dumbo ran to jump onto the top elephant—oh, no! He tripped over his big ears and bumped into the pyramid. The elephants crashed to the ground and the whole circus tent fell down around them.

Bump, bump, bump!

Now the elephants were angrier than ever with Dumbo. But the Ringmaster had another idea—Dumbo could become a clown!

So Dumbo was dressed like a baby and put at the very top of a burning building. The other clowns pretended to be firefighters. They sprayed Dumbo with water and held a hoop for him to jump into.

Poor Dumbo was terrified as he jumped. Down, down he dropped until he fell through the hoop…

…into a tub of sticky goo!

The audience cheered and roared with laughter when Dumbo landed in the goo.

But Dumbo was not happy at all.…

"We're going over to see your mother!" said Timothy to cheer up Dumbo.

Dumbo and his mother were overjoyed to see each other. Mrs. Jumbo put her trunk through the bars of her cage and cuddled her son, singing a lullaby.

But all too soon it was time for Dumbo to go. Sadly, he fell asleep, and dreamed and dreamed.…

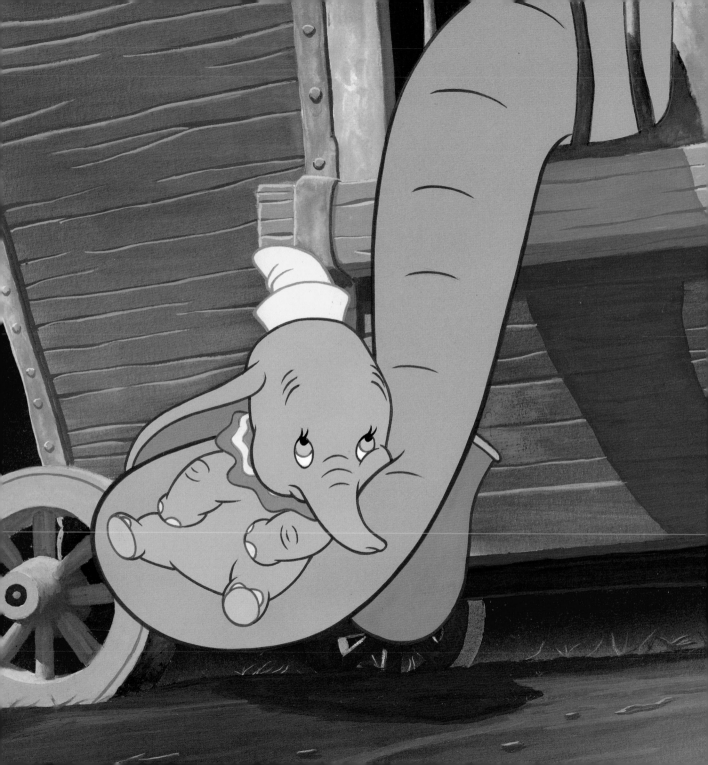

The next thing Dumbo and Timothy knew, it was morning. When they opened their eyes, they saw a group of crows looking at them.

Dumbo and Timothy were high up on the branch of a tree!

"How did they get up here?" wondered the friendly birds.

The little elephant was so surprised that he lost his balance.
Dumbo and Timothy tumbled down into a pond far below.

"I wonder how we ever got up in that tree," said Timothy,
shaking himself dry.

"Maybe you flew up!" joked one of the crows.

"Yes, that's it!" cried Timothy. "Dumbo, you *flew*!"

The little elephant looked surprised. He couldn't really fly—
could he?

Timothy told Dumbo to believe in himself.

One crow gave Timothy an ordinary feather and whispered, "Use the magic feather."

Holding the feather in his trunk, Dumbo stood at the edge of a cliff.

Before he could change his mind, the crows pushed him…

…and off he went!

All at once, Dumbo was flapping his big ears—*and he was flying!*

"Look—you're flying!" cried Timothy.

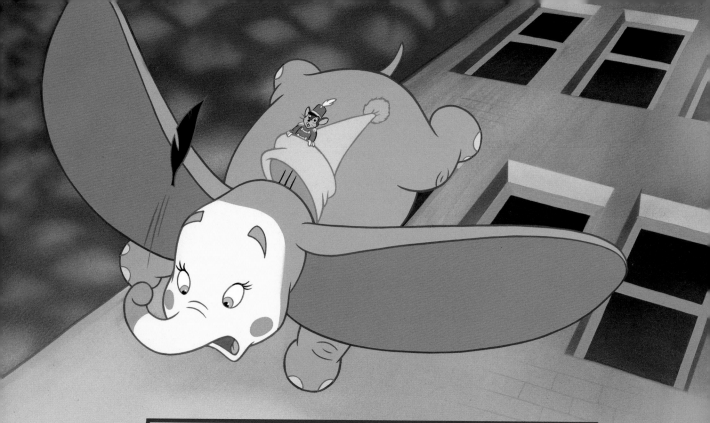

That night at the circus, Dumbo stood at the
top of the burning building. He didn't feel
frightened. Now that he had the magic feather,
he knew he could fly down safely.

Timothy was tucked inside Dumbo's hat.

"Okay," he said. "Take off!"

Just as the little elephant leaped into the air, he
dropped the feather—and Dumbo began to fall!

"Open those ears!" Timothy cried. "You *can*
fly! You *can*!"

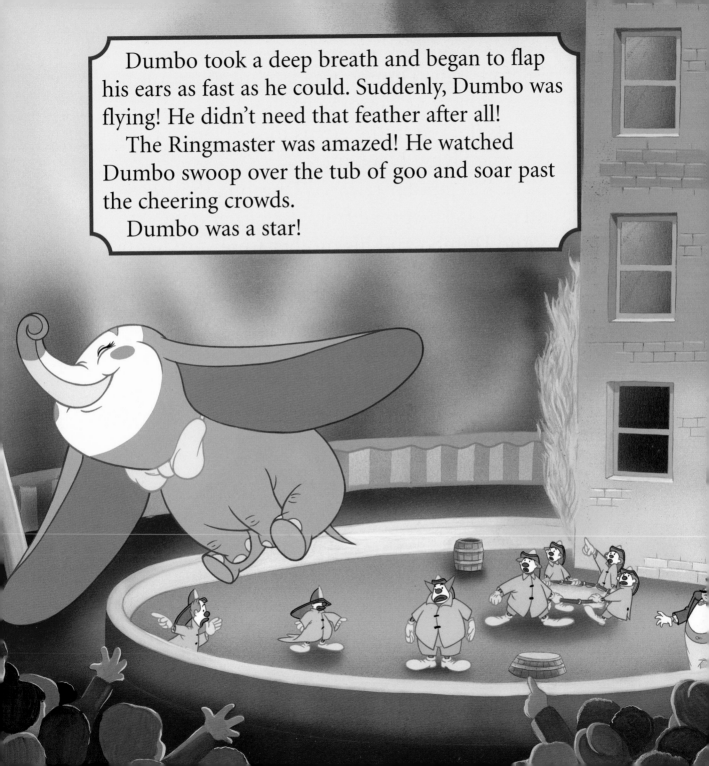

Dumbo took a deep breath and began to flap his ears as fast as he could. Suddenly, Dumbo was flying! He didn't need that feather after all!

The Ringmaster was amazed! He watched Dumbo swoop over the tub of goo and soar past the cheering crowds.

Dumbo was a star!

Before long, Dumbo was famous all around the world just as Timothy had said he would be. Crowds flocked to the circus to see "Dumbo, the Amazing Flying Elephant."

The Ringmaster released Dumbo's mother and gave her a special train car of her own.

And Dumbo and his mother were very happy.